Karen's Mistake

**Other books by
Ann M. Martin**

P. S. Longer Letter Later
(written with Paula Danziger)
Leo the Magnificat
Rachel Parker, Kindergarten Show-off
Eleven Kids, One Summer
Ma and Pa Dracula
Yours Turly, Shirley
Ten Kids, No Pets
With You and Without You
Me and Katie (the Pest)
Stage Fright
Inside Out
Bummer Summer

For older readers:

Missing Since Monday
Just a Summer Romance
Slam Book

THE BABY-SITTERS CLUB series
THE BABY-SITTERS CLUB mysteries
THE KIDS IN MS. COLMAN'S CLASS series
BABY-SITTERS LITTLE SISTER series
(see inside book covers for a complete listing)

Little Sister

Karen's Mistake

Ann M. Martin

Illustrations by Susan Crocca Tang

A
LITTLE APPLE
PAPERBACK

SCHOLASTIC INC.
New York Toronto London Auckland Sydney
Mexico City New Delhi Hong Kong

The author gratefully acknowledges
Stephanie Calmenson
for her help
with this book.

Karen's Mistake

1

Exciting Plans

It was the last week of December. I was in the den with my family playing Clue Junior. The game was a Christmas present from my stepmother, Elizabeth.

It was my turn, and I was pretty sure I had solved the mystery.

I peeked into the envelope that held the three game cards.

"I did it! I won!" I said.

"Good job!" said Daddy. "You are an excellent detective."

Excuse me while I take my bows. Okay. I

am finished. Now I can tell you who I am. My name is Karen Brewer. I am seven years old. I have blonde hair, blue eyes, and freckles. I wear glasses. I even have two pairs. I wear the blue pair for reading. I wear the pink pair the rest of the time.

"I want to play again," said Andrew, my little brother. He is four going on five.

While we were setting up for another game, Daddy said, "Does anyone have special plans for Friday night?" Friday night was New Year's Eve. I guessed that my older stepbrothers, Sam and Charlie, would have plans. They are in high school and are very popular. I guessed wrong.

"I do not have plans yet," said Charlie.

"Me neither," said Sam.

I waited to hear who my stepsister, Kristy, would be baby-sitting for. She is thirteen and the president of a baby-sitting club. But she did not have a job lined up.

"A lot of families are away for the holidays or staying home this year," she said.

My stepbrother David Michael, who is

seven like me, thought he might have plans.

"I might be sleeping at my friend Roger's house," he said. "But I am not sure. He has to ask his parents."

"How about you, Karen? Have you made any plans?" asked Nannie, my stepgrandmother.

"I would like to have a sleepover with Hannie and Nancy. But we have not decided whose house it will be at yet," I replied. (Hannie Papadakis and Nancy Dawes are my two best friends.)

"It sounds as though everyone's plans are up in the air," said Daddy. "Maybe we should do something together."

"I like that idea," said Elizabeth.

"I think we should have a party. Then anyone who has no other plans can come," said Charlie.

"It is time for a vote," said Sam. "Whoever wants to throw a party say, 'Aye!' "

There were nine "Ayes," and one "Ya-ya-ya!" That came from Emily Michelle, my little sister. She is two and a half. We decided her vote was a yes. That meant everyone in my family wanted to have a party.

"Par-ty! Par-ty!" said Andrew.

We were so excited about the plan that we forgot all about our second game of Clue Junior. Daddy and Elizabeth got busy giving us assignments. We had to shop for food, make decorations, and call our guests. Nannie promised to make her special sweets for the party. I volunteered to help. I love helping Nannie.

"We will have to work hard to be ready by Friday. It is only three days away," said Daddy.

"No problem," I said. "We can do it."

The grown-ups took another vote and decided to let everyone stay up till after midnight on New Year's Eve. (Everyone except Emily, of course. She is too young.)

Yippee! We were going to have a party. We were going to stay up past midnight. I could hardly wait to call my friends.

2

More to Tell

Hannie and Nancy thought our New Year's Eve plan was the best! But wait. I have told you about my two best friends. And I have introduced you to my big-house family. But there is something important about me I have not told you yet. The family you met is not my only family. I have a little-house family also.

That is right. I have two families. I will tell you how that happened.

A long time ago, when I was little, I had one family. It was Mommy, Daddy, Andrew, and me. We all lived together in the big house, here in Stoneybrook, Connecticut.

Then Mommy and Daddy started arguing a lot. It was no fun. They tried hard to work things out. But they could not do it. They told Andrew and me that they loved each of us very much and always would. But they could not be married to each other anymore. So they got divorced.

Mommy moved, with Andrew and me, to a little house not far away. Then she met a very nice man named Seth. She and Seth got married, and now Seth is my stepfather.

So when I am at the little house, I live with Mommy, Seth, and Andrew. Oh, yes. We have pets too. They are Emily Junior, my pet rat (you can guess who I named her after!); Bob, Andrew's hermit crab; Midgie, Seth's dog; and Rocky, Seth's cat.

Daddy stayed in the big house after the divorce. (It is the house he grew up in.) He met and married a very nice person too. That is Elizabeth, who is now my step-mother.

Elizabeth was married once before. Her four children from her first marriage are David Michael, Kristy, Sam, and Charlie.

Emily was adopted by Daddy and Elizabeth from a faraway country called Vietnam.

That is when Nannie moved into the big house. Nannie is Elizabeth's mother, which is how she became my stepgrandmother. She moved in so she could help with Emily. But really she helps everyone.

We have lots of pets at the big house. They are Shannon, David Michael's big Bernese mountain dog puppy; Pumpkin, our black kitten; Crystal Light the Second, my goldfish; and Goldfishie, Andrew's donkey. (Hee-haw! Goldfishie is Andrew's fish.)

Andrew and I switch houses almost every month. We spend one month at the big house, then one month at the little house. I gave us special names because we have two of so many things. (That makes moving back and forth a lot easier.) I call us Andrew Two-Two and Karen Two-Two. I thought up those names after my teacher read a book to our class. It was called *Jacob Two-Two Meets the Hooded Fang*.

Andrew and I have two families, with two mommies and two daddies. We have two sets of toys and clothes and books. We have two bicycles, one at each house. I have twin stuffed cats. Goosie lives at the little house. Moosie lives at the big house. And you already know about my two best friends, Hannie and Nancy. Hannie lives across the street and one house over from the big house. Nancy lives next door to the little house. We are together so much that we call ourselves the Three Musketeers.

Now you know my story. It is time to tell you more about the party.

You Are All Invited

There was not enough time to mail invitations to our party. So on Wednesday we started making phone calls. But first we made a guest list. There were friends from work and school and the neighborhood to invite. The list was very long.

"We can take turns making the calls," said Sam. "I will go first."

Sam loves to talk on the phone. Forty minutes later, the receiver was still in his hand.

"It is my turn!" I said.

"To be fair, we will pick numbers from a hat," said Elizabeth. "Each person will be allowed fifteen minutes in which to make their phone calls. After fifteen minutes, it will be the next person's turn."

Guess what. My turn came next!

I called Melody Korman and Scott Hsu, who are friends from the neighborhood. They both said they could come.

I was deciding which friend to call next when the phone rang. It was Hannie.

"Hi, Hannie! What is up?" I said.

"Um, I forgot to ask you if you wanted me to come to the party by myself or with my family," said Hannie.

"Of course your family is invited! We are inviting all our friends and neighbors," I said.

Oops. I had remembered to tell Melody and Scott that their families were invited. But I had forgotten when I called Hannie and Nancy, because I was so excited that we could stay up past midnight. It was all we talked about.

"I had better call Nancy and tell her that her parents and Danny can come," I said to Hannie.

"This is your twelve-minute warning," said Elizabeth.

Boo. I called Nancy fast. Then my time was up.

It was Elizabeth's turn. She called five people in fifteen minutes. Wow!

"I hope no one minds that I invited someone we do not know," said Elizabeth when she hung up. "Alice, my friend from work, said her father is visiting from Florida. I suggested he join us if he has no other plans."

"Of course he is welcome here. We would not want anyone to be alone on New Year's Eve," said Nannie. "But I am surprised anyone would leave warm, sunny Florida to come to Connecticut at this time of year."

While they were talking, I was busy counting up the people who would be coming to our party. There would be four people from Nancy's family. (Unless her baby brother stayed home with a sitter. Then there would be three.) There would be four people from Scott's family. There would be five people from Hannie's family and five people from Melody's family. The list kept going.

It is a good thing our house is big. We were going to have a big party!

4

Chips, Dips, and Confetti

It was Thursday. Everyone in our house was very busy. Charlie, Sam, and Kristy had gone to the supermarket to buy food for the party. Daddy and Elizabeth were hanging streamers and HAPPY NEW YEAR banners. Nannie was getting ready to bake some goodies.

"I need helpers," she said.

David Michael decided to help Daddy and Elizabeth. That left Andrew, Emily, and me to help in the kitchen. (Emily helps by banging spoons on pots to make music.)

"Andrew, will you mix the onion dip?" asked Nannie.

"Yes. I am a very good mixer," Andrew replied.

"Karen, I need you to help me measure," said Nannie. "We will start with the oatmeal and the raisins."

Yum! Making oatmeal-raisin cookies is one of my specialties. I am very good at eating them too.

I helped measure. Andrew was finished with the dip, so he helped mix. We took turns dropping spoonfuls of the batter onto baking sheets.

While the oatmeal-raisin cookies were in the oven, we started working on chocolate-chip cookies. While the chocolate-chip cookies were in the oven, we worked on the lemon squares.

That is when Kristy, Sam, and Charlie came back from the store. Their arms were filled with grocery bags. Sam and Charlie

had to run back to the car twice because there were more bags than they could carry in one trip.

"What smells so good?" asked Kristy.

"Cookies, cakes, and dips," said Andrew. "I am a good mixer!"

"You sure are," said Nannie. "Would you like to mix up a bowl of fruit punch now? Maybe Kristy will help."

"Sure I will. Come on, Andrew. It is time to make punch," said Kristy.

Andrew made two fists and poked them in the air.

"Very funny," said Kristy. "I do not think that kind of punch will help when our guests get thirsty."

Daddy popped his head into the kitchen.

"We need another confetti maker," he said.

"I will help!" I replied.

I got to work with David Michael on the living room floor. We cut brightly colored paper into little squares and triangles to make confetti. We put it into a big bowl.

Snip, snip.

Woof! Shannon raced past us. David Michael and I were extra careful with our scissors when she ran by.

Snip, snip.

Meow! Pumpkin chased Shannon. When she was gone, we went back to cutting.

Snip. Woof! Snip. Meow!

Shannon and Pumpkin raced into the kitchen. The next thing we heard was something clattering on the kitchen floor.

"No! No!" said Andrew. "They spilled the punch!"

I heard Andrew start to cry. Daddy, Elizabeth, David Michael, and I ran to the kitchen. Nannie was trying to comfort Andrew.

"Do not cry," she said. "We have plenty of fruit and juice. You can start over."

"What happened?" I asked.

"Shannon knocked into me and I knocked into Andrew while he was mixing the punch," said Kristy.

The next thing we knew, something was

18

crashing to the floor in the living room. When we got there, we saw confetti everywhere. And it was not even New Year's Eve yet!

Everyone laughed, even Andrew.

"I think we should cross Shannon and Pumpkin off our guest list," I said.

"I think you are right," agreed Daddy.

We got to work picking up confetti.

Hannie's Crush

By Thursday night we were tired, but ready for our party.

"Good night, everyone!" I said. "It is time for me to go to bed."

Lots of times someone has to push me into bed. But I knew that I needed a good night's rest on Thursday, so I would not be too sleepy at midnight on New Year's Eve.

I slept late on Friday morning. I probably would have slept longer, but I got a phone call.

"Hi, it's me," said Nancy. "I am so excited

about the party tonight. I went to bed early so I would not be too tired."

"Me too. But we are going to be having too much fun to get tired," I said. "And we will be eating so much candy and cake. All that sugar will keep us awake."

"Did you talk to Hannie this morning?" asked Nancy. "She sounded kind of funny. I wanted to talk about the party. But all *she* could talk about was the Nate Bellows concert. It is going to be on TV tonight."

Nate Bellows was a very popular singer.

"I know she loves him. She has been talking about him every day for a week. But she will love the party too," I said.

We talked about the guests, and what we would wear.

"Speaking of clothes, I had better go," I said. "It is getting late and I am still in my pajamas. Also, I want to call Hannie."

"If you are going to call, you should do it now. I think she is going out with her parents," said Nancy.

"Okay, thanks," I replied.

I called right away. Nancy was right. Hannie did sound kind of funny.

"So are you ready for the party tonight?" I asked. "Nancy and I were deciding what we would wear."

"It does not matter much to me," said Hannie. "He cannot see what I am wearing."

"What do you mean? Everyone will see what you are wearing," I replied.

"Nate Bellows will not see me. He will be giving a concert on TV. But I will see him."

"You may be a little too busy to watch TV," I said. "The only time anyone will be watching TV is at midnight, when the big ball goes down."

"I really want to watch the concert," said Hannie.

"Maybe you can watch bits and pieces of it," I said. "But you cannot watch the whole thing. You would miss the party!"

"I guess bits and pieces of Nate will be better than none of him."

Hmm.

By the time I hung up, I felt pretty annoyed at Hannie. I got dressed and went downstairs to have some breakfast. While I was eating, I told Nannie about Hannie and her crush.

"I think it would be nice for my best friend to be a little more interested in our party," I said.

"I understand how you feel," said Nannie. "But it sounds as though Hannie thinks she is in love. Being in love is a pretty wonderful thing."

"Having a New Year's Eve party and staying up till midnight is pretty wonderful too," I said. "I can hardly wait!"

6

Welcome, Mr. English

At a quarter to eight that evening, Hannie and Nancy arrived.

"I am glad you are here!" I said. "We are going to have important party jobs. Now that you are here, we can find out what they are."

"Girls, here are your assignments," said Daddy. "As our guests arrive, please take their coats and put them in our room upstairs."

"No problem!" said Nancy.

"Will you please let me know if we run low on soda or ice?" said Elizabeth.

"We can do that!" said Hannie.

"And I will need you to pass around food," said Nannie.

"We can do it all!" I replied. "The Three Musketeers are at your service."

All these important jobs were going to be fun. The whole party was going to be fun!

"Karen, I may not be able to pass food around later," said Hannie. "You know I have to watch the Nate Bellows concert."

Boo. I wished Hannie would forget about Nate Bellows and just have a good time at the party. Then I had an idea.

"We could tape the concert for you," I said.

"No, I need to watch it live," said Hannie.

Dingdong! I had no more time to talk to Hannie. Our first guests had arrived. Daddy opened the door.

"Hi, Melody!" I said.

We all greeted the Korman family. Hannie, Nancy, and I took their coats. The minute we got to the top of the stairs, the doorbell rang again. We tossed the coats on the bed in Daddy and Elizabeth's room, and ran back downstairs.

A couple of Sam's friends had arrived. More people were walking up the street, and cars were pulling up to the curb. Soon Nancy, Hannie, and I were running up and down the stairs a mile a minute.

"Karen, this would be a good time to start passing around some food," said Nannie.

My friends and I each picked up a tray. Passing food was more fun than putting away coats. I got to talk to everyone, plus I got to eat.

"I want to help," said Andrew.

"Follow me with the napkins," I said.

I gave him some napkins with balloons and party horns on them. As soon as someone took something to eat, Andrew handed out a napkin. In no time, the tray was empty.

"Wow, everyone is really hungry," said Andrew.

"You can stay here and talk to people," I said. "I will get more food."

I went to the kitchen for a refill.

"Hi, Karen," said Elizabeth. "I have another tray ready. But before you go, I would like to introduce you to Mr. English, who is my friend Alice's father. He is visiting from Florida. We want to make him feel at home."

"Hi, Mr. English," I said. I took the tray from Elizabeth and held it out to our guest. "Would you like a cracker with cheese?"

"Thank you. That looks delicious," he replied. He took one of the crackers.

"Would you like another? I have to take the tray around the whole living room, and they might go fast."

"Not right now, thank you. I will find you later," said Mr. English.

By the time I saw Mr. English again, there were just two crackers with cheese left.

"I see I found you just in time," said Mr. English.

He took one cracker. Then he took the tray from me and offered me the other cracker.

While we were munching on our crackers, Nannie passed by. I tried to be a good host to our new guest.

"Nannie, have you met Mr. English? He came here all the way from Florida," I said.

"We met for a moment in the kitchen. But I have been so busy, we have not had a chance to talk," said Nannie.

"Well, you two can talk now. I have to go get more food!" I said. "See you later."

I left Nannie and Mr. English together and went to the kitchen to refill my tray.

7

Two Musketeers

I found Hannie and Nancy in the kitchen. I was glad to see my friends. I had had enough grown-up company for awhile.

"Daddy, do you mind if we take a break from passing food?" I asked.

"Of course not. You girls have been a terrific help. Thank you very much. Now go have fun!" replied Daddy.

"Come on, we can go upstairs," I said.

"It is almost time for the concert," said Hannie. "There is a TV in the room where the coats are, right?"

"Yes, we can go there if you want," I replied.

We went to Daddy and Elizabeth's room. The pile of coats on the bed was huge.

"Watch this!" I said.

I jumped into the pile and bounced around.

"It is a coat trampoline," said Nancy. "Make room for me!"

She jumped into the pile and bounced next to me.

"Come on, Hannie," I said. "This is fun!"

"Not now. The concert is starting."

Hannie sat on the floor in front of the TV.

"Do you want to watch with me?" she asked.

"No, thank you," I said. "There is something else I want to do."

I put on a big fake fur coat. It was white with black trim.

"Oooh, you look very elegant in that," said Nancy. "I am going to try this one."

She put on an enormous red down parka.

"You look like a red marshmallow!" I said.

"Hannie, look at me!" said Nancy.

Hannie did not move an inch.

"Which is more fun? A concert on TV or your friends?" I asked.

I would have no trouble answering that question. I wanted to be with my friends. Hannie had no trouble answering either.

"This is a *Nate Bellows* concert!" she said.

Nancy and I rolled our eyes. We tried on some more coats. We were going to have fun even if Hannie was not joining us.

I put on a man's overcoat and hat. "Hello, and happy new year," I said in a deep voice.

Nancy found a baby's pink knit cap. "Goo-goo, ga-ga," she said.

"Will you please talk a little more quietly?" said Hannie.

I did not answer Hannie. I was afraid I would say something that was not very friendly. I turned to Nancy. "Who wants to go downstairs and get some cookies and candy?" I asked. "I helped Nannie make them yesterday afternoon. They are really good."

"I already had some of the cookies and they were delicious. I am ready for more," said Nancy.

"Hannie, do you want to come with us?" I asked.

"No, thank you," Hannie replied.

"We need to eat sweets. The sugar will help keep us awake for midnight," I said.

"Nate's voice is all I need to keep me awake," said Hannie.

Yuck! It was no use talking to Hannie.

"Come on, Karen. We will let Hannie stay here with Nate," said Nancy.

"That is right. The *Two* Musketeers will go downstairs and get delicious homemade goodies. See you later, Hannie!" I said.

She did not even turn around to say good-bye.

8

Midnight Surprise

Downstairs, we heard laughter coming from the den. A bunch of kids were sitting in a circle on the floor.

"Come on! We are playing Telephone," said Kristy.

"We have each had a turn already, so one of you can start," said Scott Hsu.

Nancy let me go first. I whispered in her ear, "The bear went over the mountain to see what he could see."

"This is going to be a good one," said Nancy.

She whispered what I had said into David Michael's ear. David Michael whispered it to Andrew.

"Huh?" said Andrew.

"No repeating. Just pass it around!" said Melody.

Andrew whispered into Linny's ear. (Linny is Hannie's brother. He is nine years old.)

The secret sentence went around the circle till it reached Melody. She was the last person.

"This sentence is really weird," she said. "The bear went to a fountain to see about a bee."

I was laughing so hard, I could hardly say the real sentence.

Then it was Nancy's turn. Her sentence was "Old MacDonald had a farm." The sentence turned into "Ronald McDonald had two arms"!

While we were playing, I saw Hannie come down a few times, then run back upstairs. She probably came down during the commercials. Finally the concert must have ended, because she came down and stayed.

I did not invite her to sit with us. If she would rather be with Nate Bellows than with her friends, she could find her own place to sit.

We were still having fun in the den when Daddy announced the time.

"Five minutes to midnight," he said.

"We did it! We stayed awake," I said to Nancy.

The truth was I was pretty tired, even after all the candy I had eaten. But it was not time to think about being tired. It was time for a countdown to midnight.

"Four minutes!" called Daddy.

Some more people crowded into the den to watch the ball drop on TV.

"Three minutes!" said Daddy.

The next thing I knew, we were counting down seconds instead of minutes. Everyone counted together.

"Ten! Nine! Eight! Seven! Six! Five! Four!

Three! Two! One! Happy new year!" we all shouted.

Horns blew. Our homemade confetti went flying in the air.

I was jumping up and down with Nancy when I saw Hannie looking at us. I knew that I did not want to start the new year being mad at my friend. I held out my hand for Hannie to join us.

The Three Musketeers began to jump up and down together. While we were jumping, I saw something that made my eyes open wide.

I saw Nannie being kissed on the cheek by Mr. English!

9

Life Without Nannie?

On Saturday morning I decided it had not really happened. Nannie had not been kissed by Mr. English.

"I was very tired last night, and I was probably seeing things," I whispered to Moosie. (I was whispering because my friends were still asleep.) "Maybe I just dreamed that I saw the kiss."

Moosie did not say anything. I was going to have to figure the mystery out for myself.

Hmm. Maybe I had had a cloud of confetti in my eyes. Instead of kissing her on the cheek, maybe Mr. English had been whispering in Nannie's ear. He was whispering, "Happy new year," because it was noisy and she could not hear him.

On the other hand, maybe he really did kiss Nannie. And maybe Nannie really did smile at him afterward, which is the way I remembered it. Why would she do that?

Then I remembered something else. It was a little thing, but it might be the answer to the mystery. I remembered what Nannie had said about falling in love, when I talked to her about Hannie's crush. She had said being in love is a pretty wonderful thing.

What would happen if Nannie fell in love? She would be so busy being in love that she might not have time for her family anymore. Life without Nannie would be awful.

Who would help with Emily? And Andrew? And the pets? Who would help all of us? There would be no more baking cookies. No more making prizewinning chocolates.

(Did I mention that Nannie won the Cocoa-Best cooking contest for her chocolate recipe? She did, and I helped.)

My worrying was interrupted by the sound of a yawn coming from Nancy's direction.

"Good morning," said Nancy. "What time is it?"

I decided not to tell anyone about Nannie and the kiss. Maybe if I did not say anything, the mess would disappear.

"It is time for breakfast," I replied. "I am hungry."

Hannie sat up next. "Me too," she said.

My friends and I got dressed and went down to the kitchen. We had a full house. Everyone was up except Sam and Charlie. Kristy was there with a couple of friends who had slept over. The table was covered with food. No doubt Nannie was the one who had put it on the table.

"Good morning and happy new year," said Daddy.

"How did you girls sleep?" asked Elizabeth.

"Really well," said Nancy. "We were so tired."

"Happy, happy!" said Emily.

Nannie was wiping cereal off my little sister's chin. Emily needed her Nannie! I decided to find out more about Mr. English. While everyone was talking about the party, I slipped in a few questions.

"I hope Mr. English had a good time last night," I said. "After all, he did not know anyone."

"Brian said to thank you," said Nannie. "You were an excellent host, and he had a very good time."

"I was glad he could join us," said Elizabeth. "He seems like a very nice man. He told me he lives in a big house on the beach and likes to play golf very much."

"Would anyone like more juice?" asked Nannie.

I was busy thinking about what I had learned. Mr. English's first name was Brian.

He had a big house and played golf. And Nannie did not seem to be especially interested in him this morning.

I was thinking there might not be much to worry about after all. But I was still glad that Mr. Brian English lived far away.

10

It Is a Date!

All our guests were gone by early afternoon.

"Who would like to watch our movie now?" asked Daddy.

We had decided the day before that New Year's Day would be a good time to be cozy at home together. We had rented *The Wizard of Oz*. It was fun to watch, even though everyone except Andrew and Emily had seen it lots of times before.

"Follow the yellow brick road! Follow the yellow brick road!" I sang.

I was curled up on the couch under a blanket with Kristy, David Michael, and Andrew. The movie knocked any worries I had right out of my head. It was a new year. It had come with a little bit of a shaky start. But sitting cozily under the blanket and looking at Nannie with Emily on her lap made me see that things were going to be all right.

Ring! Ring!

The telephone rang, and I jumped up to answer it. Daddy paused the movie.

"Hello?" I said.

I heard a man's voice on the other end.

"May I please speak to Janet?" asked the voice.

Uh-oh. Janet is Nannie's name. It is the name her friends call her. Old friends and new friends. New friends like Mr. English.

"Nannie, it is for you," I said.

Nannie settled Emily on Elizabeth's lap. Then she took the phone. "Hello?" she said. Then, "Just fine, Brian. How are you?"

I knew it!

Nannie waved to Daddy to start the movie again. Then she walked into the hallway with the phone.

Everyone began watching the movie again. Except me. I was not as interested in the yellow brick road as I was in the hallway.

"I will be right back," I said.

"Do you want me to stop the movie?" asked Daddy.

"No, that is okay. I am just going to the bathroom. I will be back in a minute."

I did not really have to go to the bathroom. But if I walked by Nannie slowly, I would be able to hear what she was saying.

"No, tomorrow would not work for me," said Nannie.

Uh-oh. He was asking her out!

"Monday? Yes, Monday would be fine," said Nannie.

How could she?

"Around four o'clock would be perfect," she said. "It is a date!"

I went to the bathroom and shut the door.

I sat on the closed toilet seat and put my head in my hands.

What had I done? I had brought Nannie and Brian English together. And now they had a date on Monday at four.

11

Girl Talk

While we were getting dinner ready, I heard Nannie tell Elizabeth about her plans.

"I am glad you enjoyed meeting him," said Elizabeth. "I know he will be staying with Alice till the end of the month."

When I heard that, I dropped the spoons I had been carrying to the table. They made a racket clattering to the floor. "Are you all right?" asked Elizabeth.

"Yes," I replied.

I was not about to tell Elizabeth what I was thinking. All my worries had poured back into my head. If Mr. English was going to be here for a month, that would give Nannie plenty of time to see him. The more she saw him, the more she might like him.

I returned to the kitchen to get some napkins for the table.

"Is Mr. English married?" I asked.

"He was, but his wife died about ten years ago," said Elizabeth.

I held on tight to the napkins. This was not good news. He was probably very lonely by now. He was probably looking for good company. Good company like our Nannie. But we loved Nannie. We *needed* Nannie.

I worried so much that I could hardly eat my dinner. I was glad when Hannie called and invited me to come over on Sunday afternoon. Nancy would be there too.

"I am glad," I said. "I need to talk to my friends."

The next afternoon, I told Hannie and Nancy about Nannie.

50

"What do you think?" I asked. "What if she falls in love?"

"This is only their first date," said Nancy. "Maybe you are worrying too soon."

"Maybe you are right," I said.

"I think it is good for Nannie to be dating," said Hannie. "Why should she live alone?"

"She does not live alone. She lives with her family," I replied.

"I live with my family too," said Hannie. "But I can understand why people want to be in couples. It is good to be in love. I know, because of how I feel about Nate Bellows."

I could see our talk about Nannie was over. Once Hannie started talking about Nate Bellows, it would be hard to talk about anything else.

"How can you be in love when you have never even met him?" asked Nancy.

"I have not told you this yet, but I have been writing to him every day," said Hannie. "And he has written back."

"Do you have his letters?" I asked.

"He only wrote to me once so far. But I have the letter right here," said Hannie.

She opened her drawer and passed an envelope to us. Nancy and I looked at the letter together. A picture of Nate Bellows was at the top, and some information about his life and music was below.

"This is a form letter," said Nancy.

"No way," said Hannie. "He was just too busy to write me a long letter because of his concert schedule. But that envelope has my name on it, and it came to me from Nate Bellows!"

"The same letter was probably sent to a lot of his fans," I said.

"You do not understand at all," said Hannie.

And she put the letter away.

12

Karen's Warning

On Monday my friends and I went back to school. I love school and my teacher, Ms. Colman, but it is sometimes a little hard going back to class after a holiday. It was especially hard this time, because my mind was on important things. Like Nannie's first date.

I was glad when the day was over and I could go home. But I did not feel so good about being at home when I saw Nannie all dressed up. She was wearing pearl earrings with a matching necklace, a sweater and skirt, and shoes with high heels. I tried not to be a meanie-mo.

"You look very nice," I said.

"Thank you," Nannie replied. "Would you like a snack?"

"Yes, I am hungry."

I was glad Nannie was acting like herself, even if she was dressed up. She gave me cream cheese on crackers and carrot sticks with dip that was left over from our party. Andrew and Emily were having the same thing. I was crunching a carrot when the doorbell rang.

Nannie answered it and brought Mr. English in to say hello. He was dressed up too. But I did not tell him he looked nice.

Before they left, Daddy came into the kitchen. (He has an office at home where he works most of the time.)

"I will watch the kids," said Daddy. "Enjoy yourselves."

"I will not get Janet home too late," said

Mr. English. "We are going to do some shopping and have an early-bird dinner downtown."

I ran to the window and watched them drive away.

Then I finished my snack and went upstairs to do my homework. My mind wandered a few times. I wondered what stores Nannie and Mr. English were shopping in. Then it was back to math. And spelling.

I stopped to have dinner, then returned to my homework. It seemed like forever before I heard a car pulling into the driveway. I ran to my window and watched Nannie get out. I wanted to see if she was smiling. That would tell me if she had had a good time.

She was smiling, and that was not all. She and Mr. English were holding hands as they walked to our front door.

I could see this first date would not be the last.

I ran downstairs.

"Thank you again," I heard Nannie say

when the door opened. "I had a lovely time."

I was not the only one who had come downstairs. My whole family was there. Everyone seemed so happy for Nannie. I could not understand it. Didn't they know what might happen?

I followed Kristy to her room.

"Kristy, I want to know why you are not upset. Nannie just had her first date with Mr. English. If she keeps having a good time, she might hardly be here at all!" I said.

"Did you see how happy she was?" asked Kristy. "I hope she goes out more. We can take care of ourselves."

I talked to Sam and Charlie next. They thought the same thing.

Elizabeth seemed the happiest of all. Maybe she was just pretending. I found her sitting in the den with Daddy.

"I am worried about Nannie. She went out with Mr. English, but she hardly knows him," I said.

"I have been hearing about him from my

friend Alice for years. I know he is a very nice man," Elizabeth replied.

"But what if Nannie goes out with him all the time? What will happen to us?" I asked.

Daddy put his arm around me.

"You worry too much sometimes," he said. "Mr. English is a nice man. Nannie had a pleasant evening with him. That is all."

For now, I thought. For now.

13

What Kind of New Year Is This?

On Tuesday evening Nannie went out again. Thank goodness she did not go out with Mr. English. She went to a community meeting.

"You are going out a lot lately," I said.

"It is good to keep busy," said Nannie.

I did not tell her I did not want her to keep *too* busy.

As I watched Nannie walk down the driveway to her car, I thought of the nights I might be without her. She would not be around to read, or talk, or watch TV with me. She would not be around to help out with Emily. That meant that Elizabeth and Daddy would be busier and would have less time for me.

I was thinking of all this, trying my best to be brave, when I heard Daddy and Elizabeth talking about something very interesting. And a little scary.

"David Michael's and Kristy's schools will be closed next month for a week," said Elizabeth. "Do you think it would be a good time to take a trip to Florida?"

"It sounds like a great idea to me," said Daddy.

It did not sound so great to me. In fact, it sounded awful! I did not like thinking of the five of them going off and leaving me.

Andrew and I would be at the little house then, so we would not be able to go with them. And I did not think Sam and Charlie would go, because they had so much to do at home. But what about Nannie? Maybe she would go with them. After all, Mr. English would be back in Florida by then.

I had been standing just outside the kitchen. Now I stepped inside.

"Hi, how are you?" I said.

I did not tell Daddy and Elizabeth I had been listening to their conversation. I hoped they would say something about it. Then I could tell them what I thought. But they did not.

"Would you like to help us clean up? You can dry some bowls for us," said Daddy.

"I have homework," I replied.

I did not really think I had much homework left. But just because Nannie was out on the town did not mean I had to dry bowls. Kristy walked in then.

"I will help," she said.

Then Sam and Charlie showed up. And David Michael. Soon everyone was helping to clean up. I was still standing there.

"I thought you had homework to do," said Daddy.

"Maybe I have time to clean up *and* do my homework," I said.

"We do not want you to have to rush,"

said Elizabeth. "You should go upstairs and get to work. Thank you anyway."

Boo. I was being sent upstairs to do homework I did not have. I was going to be left out all over again.

But this time I did not really mind. I did not want to stay and help, because I was feeling sad and grumpy. Nannie was going out all the time. Daddy and Elizabeth were going to Florida. I was being left out all over the place.

The new year was not starting out very well. I was mad at everybody and everything.

14

Second Date

Guess who went out again on Wednesday night. If you guessed Nannie and Mr. Brian English, you are right. This time they went to a movie and dinner.

While they were out, I was upstairs trying to do my homework. (This time I really had some.) But all I could think about was Florida. I remembered what Nannie said about being in warm Florida instead of cold Connecticut in the winter.

Then I started thinking about Nannie and

her date. She was probably having a great time.

I looked down at my homework and a spelling word caught my eye. The word was *leave*. I had to put the word in a sentence. That was easy. I wrote, *Please do not leave!*

I had just finished writing the exclamation point when I heard a car pull into the driveway. I ran to the top of the stairs. A few seconds later I heard Nannie's voice. "Would you like to come in for coffee?" she said.

"Thank you for asking. But I promised Alice I would be home early," Mr. English replied.

I was glad to hear that. But then I heard something I was not so happy about.

"We will have to talk more about Florida," said Mr. English.

"Yes," said Nannie. "I really want — "

Suddenly I could not hear a word they were saying. Someone had turned the TV on in the den. The voices on the TV drowned out Nannie.

"Andrew! You need to press the down arrow right here," I heard Daddy say. "That will make the sound lower."

But the sound grew louder.

"Try again," said Daddy over the TV noise. "You must have pressed the up arrow."

A few seconds later I could hear Nannie's voice again. She was at the end of a sentence, and all I heard were two words. The words were *white dress*.

"Excellent," said Mr. English. "Thank you again for a lovely evening. May I call you tomorrow?"

"Of course," said Nannie.

I had to hold on to the railing so I would not fall down. When I was sure Brian was gone, I raced back to my room and threw myself on my bed. Of course Brian would call Nannie tomorrow. They would probably talk to each other every day now. I was surprised they were not talking every hour. Every minute!

"Oh, Moosie! We are going to have to say good-bye to Nannie soon," I said.

I almost began to cry. Of course Nannie was going to Florida. Brian English was there. Half my family was going. There would be a *white dress*. And a *white dress* could mean only one thing.

Nannie was going to get married in Florida, and I was not going to be there.

15

Wedding Plans?

At recess the next day, I called an emergency meeting with Hannie and Nancy on the playground. We needed to do some serious talking.

"Do you think Nannie would really get married without inviting me?" I asked.

I had gone over every detail with them, starting with how I foolishly brought Nannie and Mr. English together at the New Year's Eve party.

"Do not blame yourself. You said they had already met," said Nancy.

"But I introduced them again. And I told them to talk to each other," I said.

"It probably would have happened anyway," said Hannie. "Love is like that."

Nancy and I rolled our eyes in Hannie's direction. We could tell a Nate Bellows conversation was coming. But Nancy had more to say about Nannie first.

"In my opinion, you are jumping to conclusions," she said. "You have no proof that Nannie is getting married."

"She does not need proof. When someone is in love, you can see it in their eyes," said Hannie.

"Her eyes look exactly like they always do," I replied. "But I still think she is getting married."

"If they are getting married, I bet they will have a small, romantic wedding. That is what I want when I marry Nate Bellows," said Hannie.

"That is ridiculous!" said Nancy. "You do not even know Nate Bellows."

"Nannie only met Mr. English a few

times, and look how fast things are happening," said Hannie. "And anyway, I will be meeting Nate Bellows very soon."

"Oh, really? How are you going to do that?" asked Nancy.

"You know I have been writing to him every day. And I have a stack of letters from him," said Hannie.

"The one answer we saw was a form letter," I said.

"It was not. And neither is this invitation to his next appearance. He is going to be at Washington Mall," said Hannie.

Nancy and I looked at the so-called invitation. It was nothing personal. It was a flier.

"This notice was sent to everyone on his mailing list," I said.

"You are just jealous," said Hannie. "But I understand. It will be hard when your grandmother and your best friend get married at almost the same time."

"Hannie, you are dreaming! You have to know you are not going to marry Nate Bellows. He is a superstar, and you do not even know him," said Nancy. "You are also a little young to get married."

"Okay, I may have to wait a few years. But it will happen. I am going to meet him tomorrow at the performance he invited me to. Do you want to come?" asked Hannie.

Nancy and I looked at each other. What could we do? Our friend needed us. She needed us to help her see the real and true story. So the next day the Three Musketeers would go to Washington Mall.

16

Nannie's Secret

When I got home, Nannie had an excellent snack waiting for me. It was her homemade pizza crackers. (She puts cheese and tomato sauce on the crackers, then pops them in the oven. Yum!)

After our snack Nannie and Andrew decided to play a game of Chutes and Ladders. I was glad Nannie was acting like her old self. She did not have one single plan to go out later.

I did not feel like playing the game, but I kept them company so I could talk to Nannie. Maybe I would find out more about her wedding plans.

"It is your turn, Andrew," said Nannie.

Andrew spun the spinner.

"Hannie asked Nancy and me to go with her to see Nate Bellows at Washington Mall tomorrow," I said. "She thinks she is going to marry him."

"I had crushes on stars when I was young too," said Nannie.

"Hannie is already planning her wedding," I said.

I was trying to keep Nannie on the subject. But she did not answer. She was watching Andrew move his piece around the board. I tried again.

"Do you want to know what kind of wedding she is planning to have?" I asked.

"I am sure it is something nice," said Nannie.

"Nannie, it is your turn," said Andrew.

Nannie spun the spinner. I could see she was not going to talk to me about any wedding plans. She was being very secretive. I went upstairs to my room.

A little while later, I heard Nannie talking to Daddy. I heard him say the word *limousine*.

That did it! Nannie did not want to tell me about her wedding, but I had my proof now. White dress. Limousine. You cannot fool me!

Then Nannie called to me and said she needed help. I thought, finally she is going to tell me everything. She was going to invite me to be her flower girl, of course. (I have been a flower girl two times, so I know all about it.)

I was wrong. Nannie did not say one word about her wedding. She just wanted me to set the table. While I was putting the napkins out, Andrew said to me, "I will do that. Napkins are *my* job, remember?"

"No, I do not remember," I replied. "Nannie asked me to set the table, so that is what I am doing."

"I want to put the napkins down."

"No," I replied.

"Yes."

"No."

Andrew tried to take one of the napkins, but I held on. It was paper, so it ripped in half.

"Now look what you did!" I shouted.

"Karen, please do not shout. Use your indoor voice," said Nannie. "And it would be nice if you let Andrew help. He can put the napkins down, and you can do everything else."

I let Andrew put the napkins down. But I was not happy.

Later, when Nannie was saying good night to me, she pointed out that my room was a mess.

"It would be nice if you tried to be a bit neater," said Nannie. "Maybe you can pick up part of the mess each day."

"All right, I will try," I replied.

Nannie left, and I suddenly had a new worry. I worried that Nannie was keeping her wedding and moving plans secret only from me. I was sure that everyone else in the house knew all about her plans. She was keeping them secret from me because she did not want me to be part of them. She did not want someone who talked in a loud voice and kept a messy room at her wedding.

17

Love Connection

The last thing I wanted to do on Friday afternoon was go to the Nate Bellows concert. I did not think his music was so great. And I knew the mall would be *very* crowded. (I do not like getting pushed around in crowds.) But I had promised Hannie I would go.

"I am so excited! I am finally going to meet my true love," Hannie said to Nancy and me.

"And I am going to get my toes stepped on," I said.

"Please stay close to me, girls," said Mr. Papadakis.

Hannie's father had left work early and was leading us through the huge crowd of fans at Washington Mall.

"Keep going, Daddy. I want to be right up front," said Hannie.

"I am doing my best," Mr. Papadakis replied.

This was not a regular concert. Nate Bellows was on a promotional tour. He would sing a few of his most popular songs and then sign autographs. As we moved through the crowd, we listened to him sing "Love Connection."

Ooh, ooh!
When I met you
I just knew
It was meant to be
Just you and me.
Ooh, ooh!

I did not like the song much, but I could not help thinking of Nannie and Brian English. I wondered if they had known it was meant to be when they met.

"Did you see? He looked right at me when he sang that song," said Hannie.

"He could have been looking at any one of us," said Nancy. "And how could that song be about you? You have not met yet."

"We have met in our hearts and our letters," said Hannie.

She motioned for us to be quiet. He was introducing a brand-new song from his soon-to-be-released CD. It was called "Yes to Love."

Hey, sweet baby, I got your letter.
Nothing else could make me feel better
Than to hear from my sweet baby,
Saying yes to me, not maybe
Saying yes to love, to love, to love —
Saying yes to loving me!

I thought Hannie was going to faint.

"Can you believe it? He is writing about our letters!" she said.

I was glad Mr. Papadakis was standing off to the side. I did not think it would have made him happy to hear Hannie talking this way about someone she did not even know.

Nate Bellows sang a couple more songs. Then his manager announced that he would sign autographs.

Hannie raced to be first in line, and we followed. A couple of other fans got there before us, but Hannie's turn came fast.

"Hello, Nate," she said. "I am Hannie Papadakis. I am so happy to finally meet you!"

Nate Bellows did not even look up. He signed a flier and handed it to Hannie.

"Nate? It is me, Hannie. I saved every one of your letters. I love the new song you wrote about us," she said.

"I am glad you liked the concert," said Nate Bellows. "Be sure to buy the new CD. Next, please!"

Nate Bellows had no idea who Hannie was. Nancy and I noticed that all he had written on the flier was his own name. He had not written "Dear Hannie." He had not written a personal note.

And the flier was the same "letter" she had received in the mail. Poor Hannie!

18

Brokenhearted

I put my hand on Hannie's shoulder.

"Come on, it is time to go home," I said.

Nancy and I did not wait to get Nate Bellows's autograph. He had no idea who Hannie was, and he had not been very nice to her. Nancy and I could have said, "We told you so." But neither one of us did. Our friend, Hannie, was sad. She even started to cry a little in the car.

"Is everything all right back there?" asked Mr. Papadakis.

Hannie could not keep her tears in any

longer. She cried loudly and told her father about writing to Nate Bellows.

"I thought he was writing back to me," she said.

"I am sorry your feelings are hurt," said Mr. Papadakis. "Stars like Nate Bellows rarely have time to answer letters themselves. Usually they do not even get to see the letters. It is nothing personal. They are just too busy."

When we were back in Stoneybrook, Mr. Papadakis said Nancy and I could visit for awhile. Hannie marched straight to her room and we followed. She was not crying anymore. She was angry.

"Good-bye forever, Nate Bellows!" she said.

She tore his poster off the wall. Then she took out a shoe box filled with papers. They were all the "letters" she had received. Together we tore them up into little bits.

"Take that! And that!" said Hannie. "I am never falling in love again! It hurts too much."

"You sound like a Nate Bellows song," I said. "Remember the one called 'Hurts So Bad'?"

"It hurts to listen to that song," said Nancy. (She does not like Nate Bellows's music either.)

"This taught me a good lesson about love," said Hannie. "The lesson is to keep away from it!"

"I do not think all love hurts," said Nancy. "You just have to pick a better person."

"Maybe you are right," said Hannie. She was losing steam. She was not crying or mad. She was starting to sound like Hannie again.

All this made me think of Nannie. I began to wonder if it was hard for her to be in love too. I did not think so. At least not because of Mr. English. But maybe I was making things hard for her.

I had been feeling very sorry for myself. I had been thinking about how I would feel, losing Nannie, instead of thinking about

Nannie being happy. It was time to fix some things.

Even if Nannie moved away, and even if she decided to leave me out of the wedding, I did not want to hurt her. I needed to forgive Nannie.

It was the perfect plan for getting my new year back on track.

19

Karen's Mistake

I ate dinner at Hannie's house, then went home. I felt much better because of my new attitude. I also had a very good plan.

I was going to be grown-up and face my problem straight on. I was going to talk to Nannie.

Even though it was Friday night, Nannie was home. (I had heard her say that Alice and her father were going to a show in New York City.)

I knocked on Nannie's bedroom door.

"Come in," she said.

She was on her bed reading.

"May I talk to you for a minute?" I asked.

"Of course," Nannie replied. She put her book down and took off her glasses. Then she patted the bed beside her. "Come sit down."

I sat next to Nannie and drew in a big breath. I needed to talk fast because I had a lot to say and did not want to forget anything.

"I am sorry I have been in a funny mood lately," I said. "It really is okay that you are getting married. I hope everyone will have a wonderful time at your wedding. And I do not want love to be hard for you. I want you to be happy."

There. I had done it. I thought I had done a pretty good job too. That is why I was surprised at the expression on Nannie's face. She looked as if she had not understood a word I had said.

"Karen, what are you talking about? Who is getting married?" asked Nannie.

"You do not have to keep the secret any

longer," I replied. "I can see how you feel about Mr. English. And I heard you talking about the white dress and the limousine. I know you are getting married in Florida."

"My goodness. I had no idea you thought I was getting married," said Nannie. "I am *not*. The white dress is for a friend of mine who lives in Florida. It is a favorite dress that does not fit me anymore, and I know she would like it. The limousine is going to take everyone to the airport when we go to Florida. It is not for a wedding party. And while I like Mr. English very much, the only plan we have when I am in Florida is to play a round of golf together."

Wow. Nannie had even more to say than I had. She said it all slowly and I understood every word. But it took a minute for it to sink in.

"Does that mean you are not in love with Mr. English?" I asked.

"He is a nice man and I enjoy his company. But I do not know him very well yet. And I am in no hurry to marry. I am very

happy with the family I have," said Nannie. She gave me a hug and said one more thing I was happy to hear. "If I ever get married, you will be an important part of my wedding party, Karen. I would not have it any other way."

I gave Nannie an even bigger hug back.

20

Happy New Year, After All

I woke up on Saturday to the sound of snowflakes brushing against my window. I looked out my window and saw the snow piling up in the yard. Yippee! My new year was turning out to be pretty great, after all. There were no snowy mornings like this in Florida. I love Connecticut in the winter!

Knock, knock.

"Come in!" I said.

"I want to make a snow fort!" said Andrew. "Will you help me?"

"I will get dressed and meet you down-stairs," I replied.

Delicious smells were coming from the kitchen. Waffles. And syrup. And coffee. (I do not drink coffee but I like the smell.) I walked downstairs to the kitchen.

"Come have breakfast," said Nannie. "Then you can go outside."

There was no way I was passing up Nannie's waffles. Andrew wanted some too.

While we were eating, the doorbell rang. Once. Twice. Someone wanted us to answer in a hurry.

Sam opened the door and let Hannie in.

"Would you like to join us for some waffles?" asked Nannie.

"No, thank you. I can only stay a minute. I have to show Karen something," Hannie replied.

She held out a shiny new magazine. It was open to a picture of Josh By-Gosh. I had heard his name on the radio all week.

"He is so cute!" said Hannie.

"You thought Nate Bellows was cute too," I reminded her.

"Who needs Nate Bellows when there is Josh By-Gosh," said Hannie. "I am in love!"

I could not believe what I was hearing. "I thought you said you were never going to fall in love again."

"I never expected there would be someone like Josh," said Hannie. "Do you want to come over and help me write a letter to him? Maybe he will read it and write back to me."

"I am sorry, but I cannot come over. I promised Andrew I would build a snow fort with him," I replied.

"Okay, I will talk to you later," said Hannie.

After she left, I told Nannie about Hannie and her broken heart.

"That was just yesterday, and now she is in love again," I said.

"Love is unpredictable. It can be painful. It can be wonderful," said Nannie. "The one thing I can say is that the real thing is worth looking for."

"Hey, Karen? Are you finished talking about mushy love stuff? Can we go outside?" asked Andrew.

I looked at Andrew and at Nannie. I loved them and the rest of my family very much. I loved my friends too. For now that was enough love for me.

"Come on," I said to my little brother. "We have a snow fort to build."

L. GODWIN

About the Author

ANN M. MARTIN lives in New York City and loves animals, especially cats. She has two cats of her own, Gussie and Woody.

Other books by Ann M. Martin that you might enjoy are *Stage Fright*; *Me and Katie (the Pest)*; and the books in *The Baby-sitters Club* series.

Ann likes ice cream and *I Love Lucy*. And she has her own little sister, whose name is Jane.

BABY-SITTERS
Little Sister

Don't miss #118

KAREN'S FIGURE EIGHT

I skated near the red cones and watched out of the corner of my eye. Coach Brown was not there anymore, but Jillian was practicing her sit spins. She waved at me when she finished her spin.

"Hi, Karen!" she said.

"Hi, Jillian!" I called back proudly.

Jillian skated over to the red cone where I was standing. I could not believe it. She wanted to talk to me again!

"How was your lesson, Karen?" Jillian asked.

I told Jillian all about the crossovers. I even told her that Mrs. Harris's class was easy, because I knew how to do the moves already.

"Well, maybe I can teach you something

trickier. Do you know how to do a waltz jump?" Jillian said.

I did not know. So Jillian showed me. She leaped up and turned so gracefully. Jillian showed me how to bend my knees going into the jump and hold my arms. "And remember to keep your head up," she added.

As we skated in the red-cone area, I felt so special. Especially when I looked up and saw Kelly and Alyse watching.

I did another waltz jump and Jillian clapped. She was a great teacher.

"Your class will probably learn this in a few weeks," Jillian said. "I loved doing these when I was your age."

Jillian was teaching me some of her favorite moves!

Free skate was almost over. I could not believe how much time Jillian had spent with me. Maybe Kristy was right and Jillian really needed a friend. She probably did not see many kids her age. I could be her friend. After all, I was going to be a star skater just like her.

BABY·SITTERS™

Little Sister

by Ann M. Martin
author of The Baby-sitters Club®

More Titles... ➡